La La La

This story started with my sketching a very small, very lonely, very uncertain circle. And then a big circle appeared way up high above the small circle. The little circle was utterly charmed by the big circle — but it was so far away! How could they connect?

I played with those circles for a long time.

Finally, I figured that what the small circle needed to do was sing. Because even if we are small and alone and afraid, if we sing, sometimes someone answers us back.

And look! I was right! Because here is Jaime Kim's beautiful art answering my small, tentative song.

— Kate DiCamillo

Just like the girl in this book, I also had a time during my childhood when I felt lonely. Because of my timid and quiet nature, I had few friends and found it difficult to step outside of my own private world. Then one day my little sister was born. I still remember when my mom let me hold her for the first time. It was an unforgettable moment. While I was illustrating this story, I thought of that memory and tried to capture the relief, the overwhelming emotion, and the joy of finding the most precious friend in the world. I completed each illustration with the sincere wish that the little girl in the story would no longer be lonely. I hope all of those who read this book will find their way out of loneliness too, just like me and the little girl. I dedicate this book to my little sister, Soma, who will always be a lifelong friend of mine.

—Jaime Kim

For Karen Lotz, who believes in the song
K. D.

For my little sister, Soma
J. K.

First edition 2017

Library of Congress Catalog Card Number pending
ISBN 978-0-7636-5833-5

17 18 19 20 21 22 LEO 10 9 8 7 6 5 4 3 2 1

Printed in Heshan, Guangdong, China

This book was typeset in Caflisch Script Pro.
The illustrations were created using watercolor, sumi ink, and digital techniques.

Candlewick Press
99 Dover Street
Somerville, Massachusetts 02144

visit us at www.candlewick.com